I0830740

Sticky Graphic Novels
SLY
Dale Lazarov & mpMann

SLY

Script and art direction by Dale Lazarov
Linework and colors by mpMann
©2016 Dale Lazarov & mpMann. All rights reserved.

StickyGraphicNovels.com

Printed and distributed by
ComicMix, LLC.
71 Hauxhurst Ave.
Weehawken, NJ 07086
http://www.comicmix.com

Hardcover ISBN: 978-1-939888-54-9

SMOOTH EXTRACTION

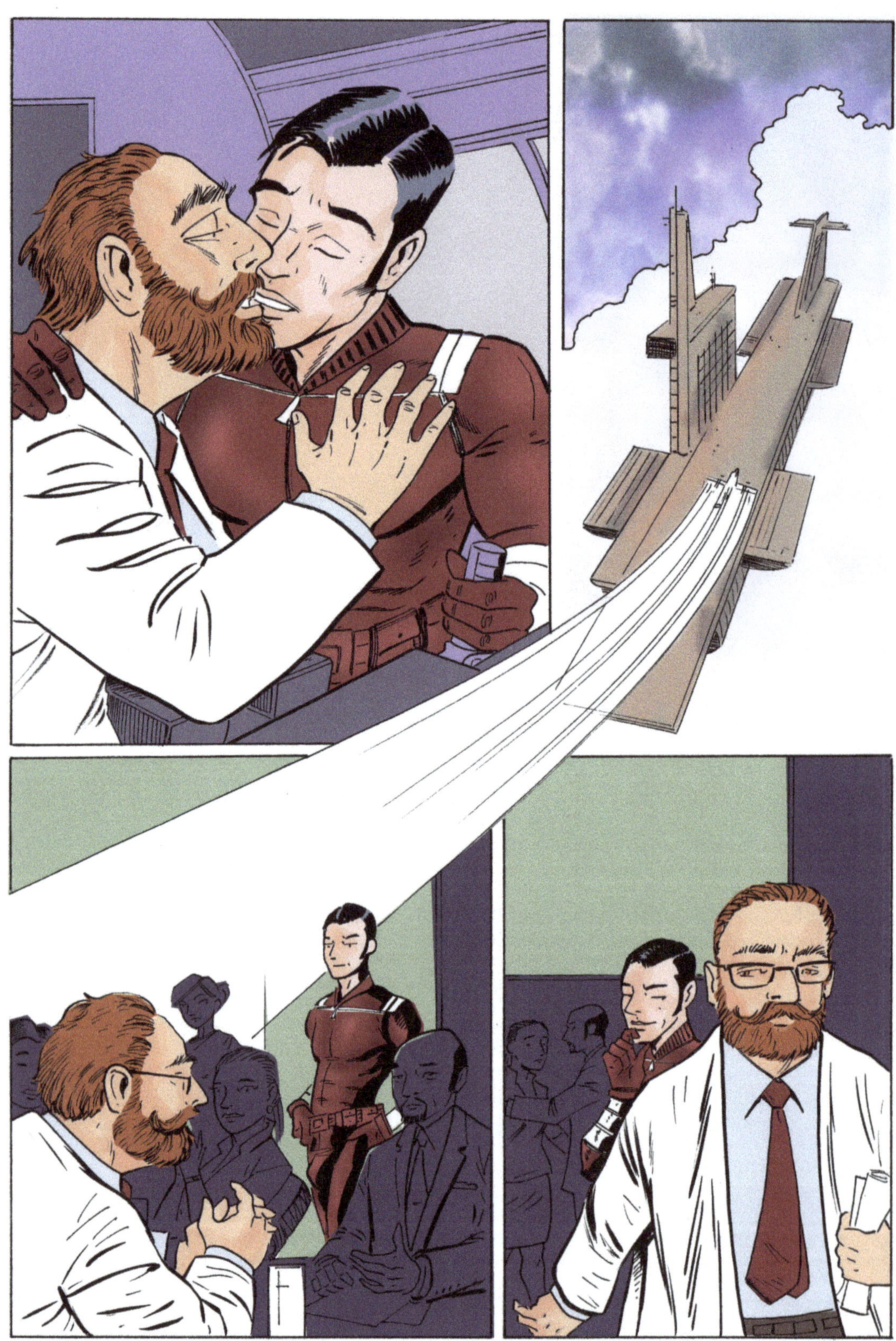

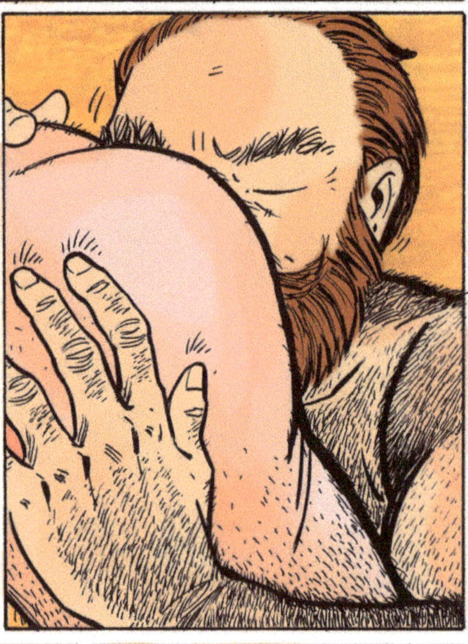
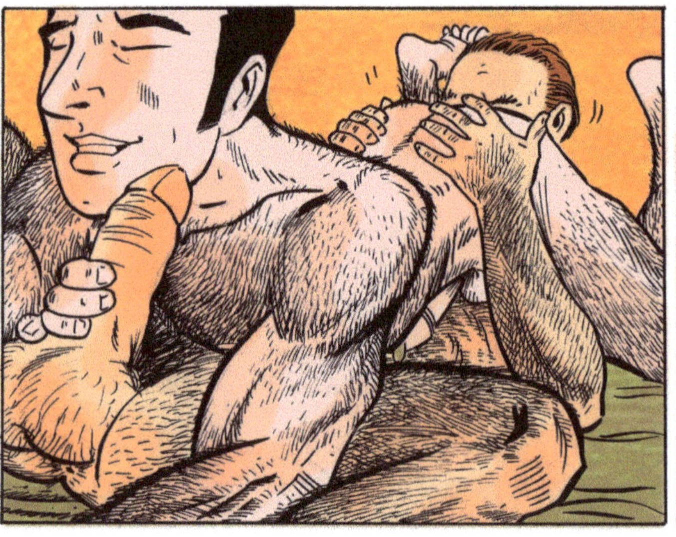
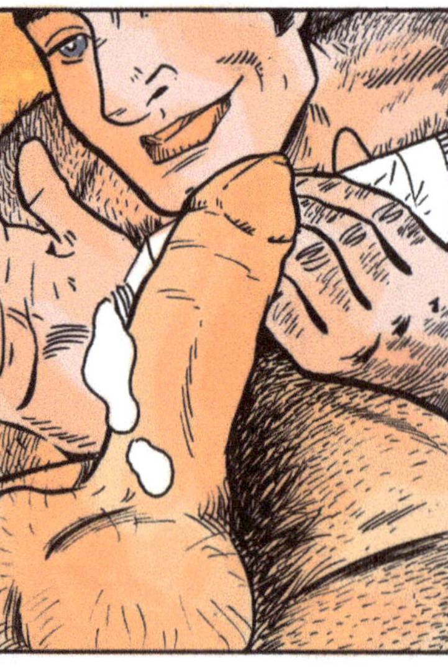

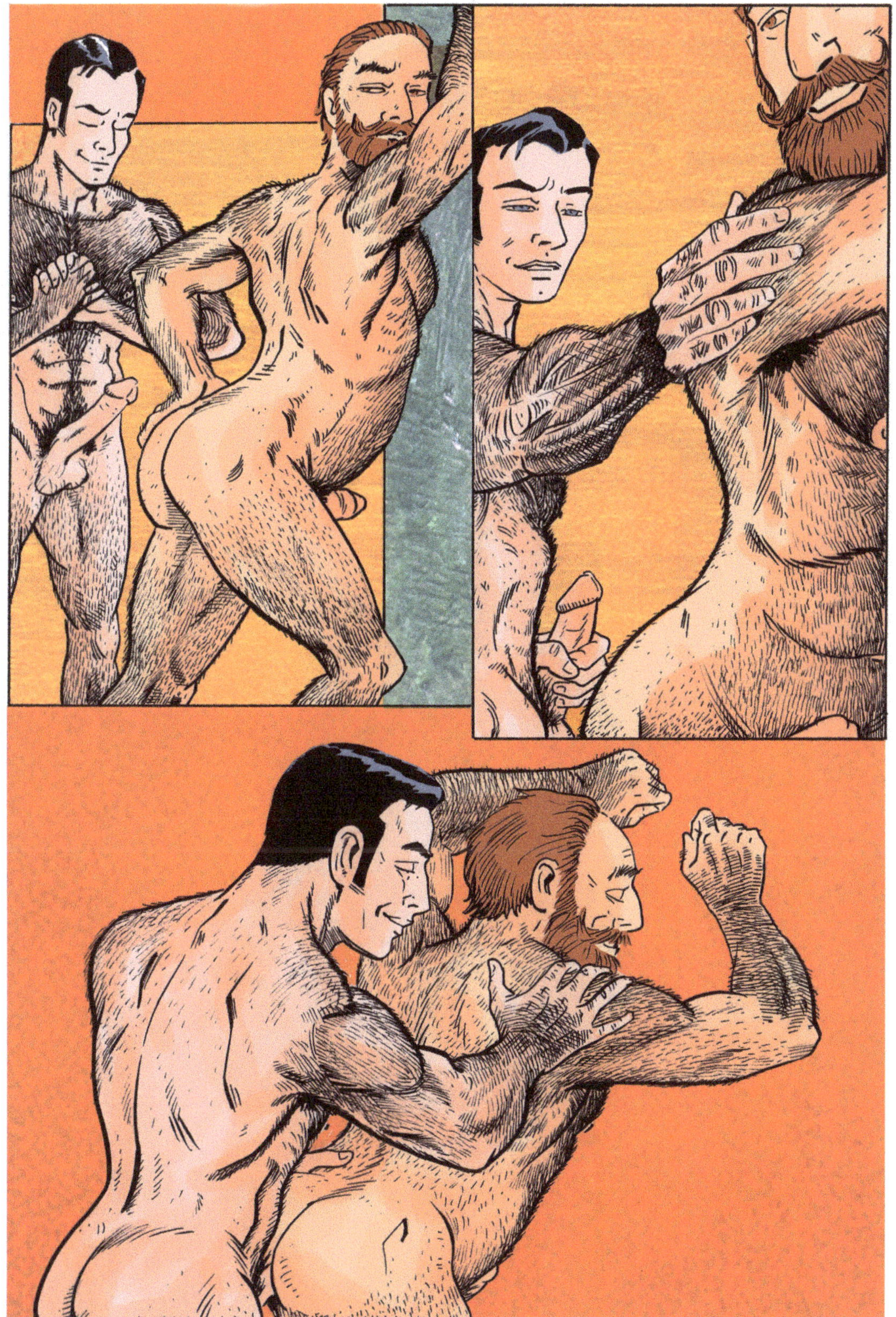

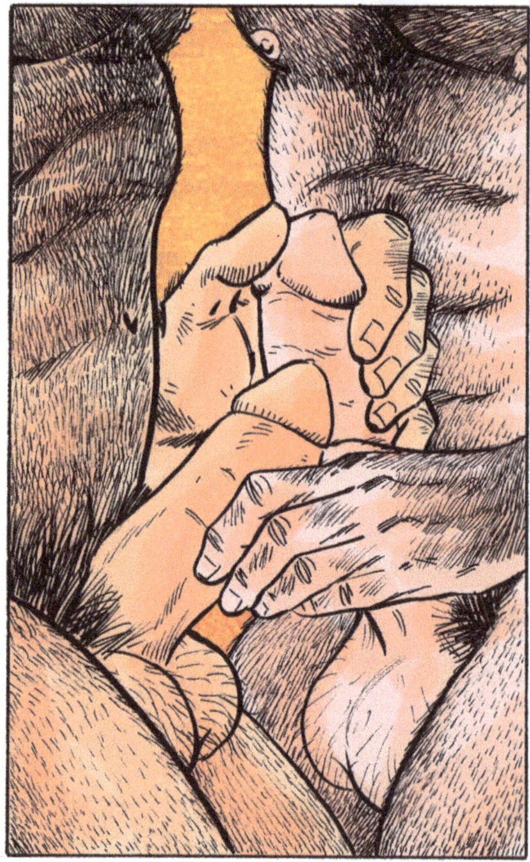

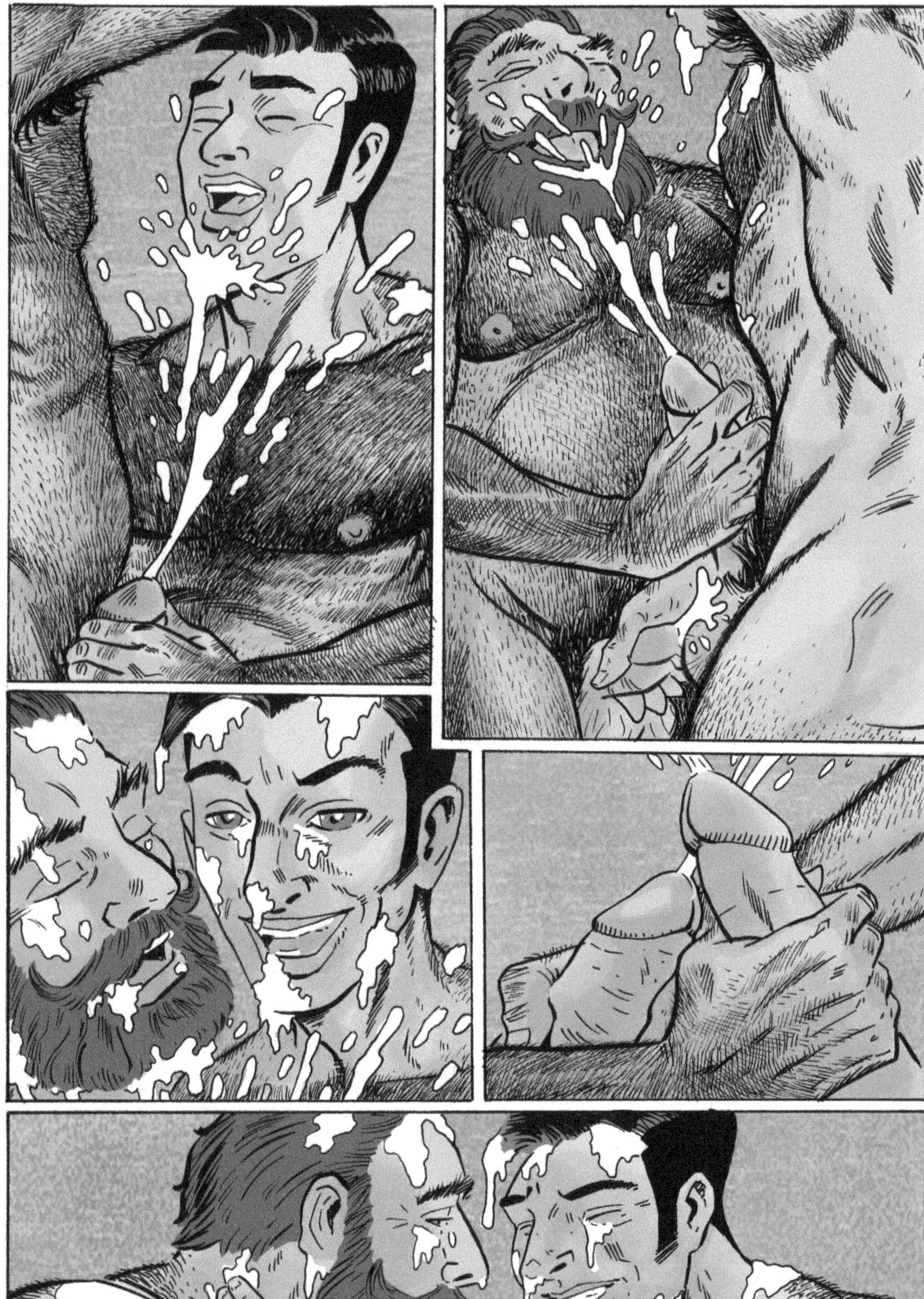

LONG-DISTANCE RELATIONSHIP

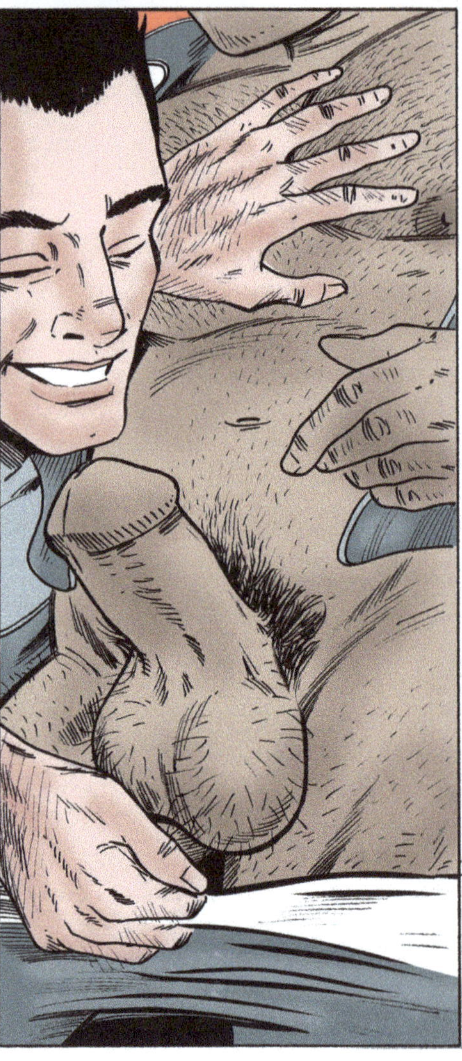

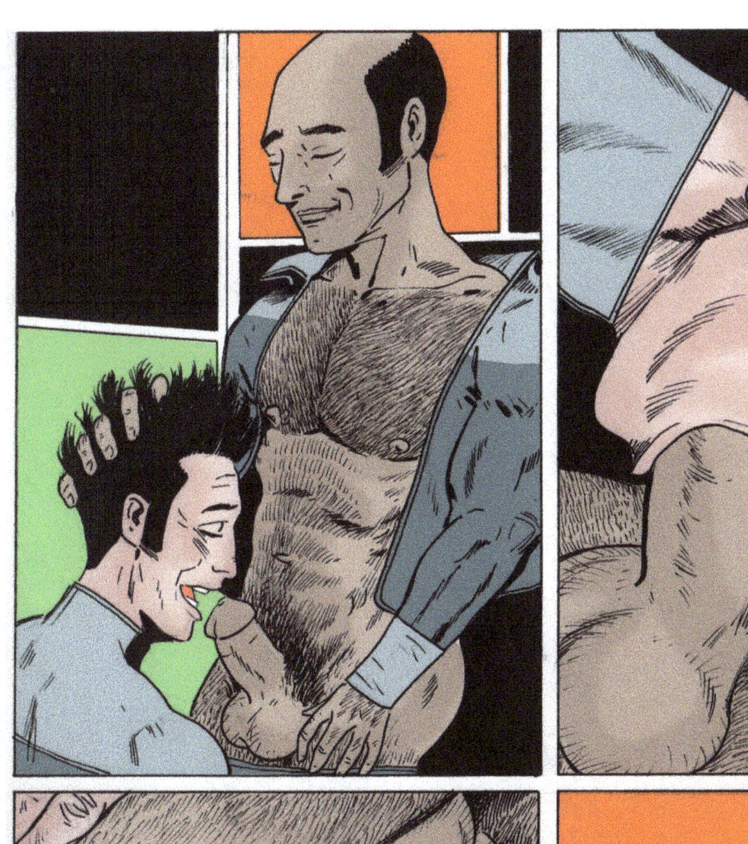
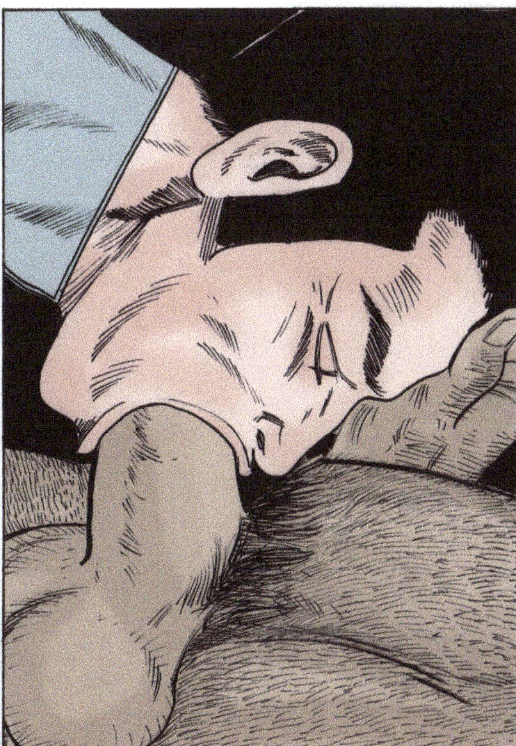

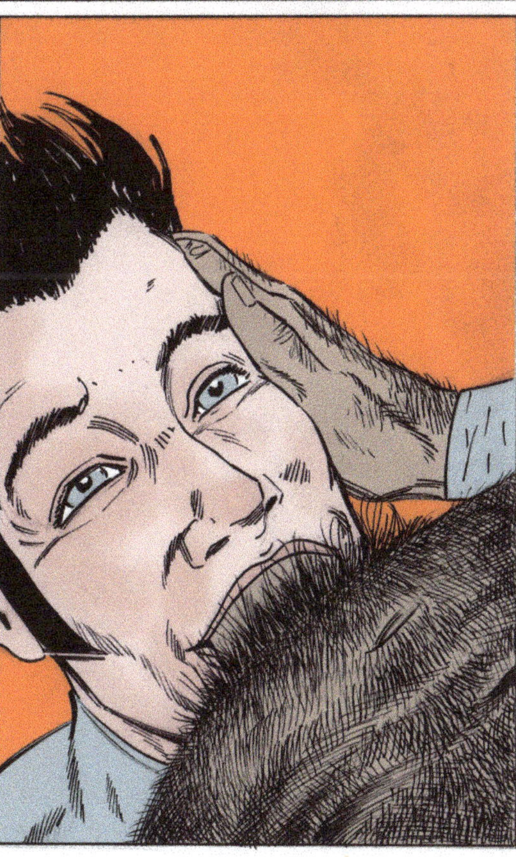

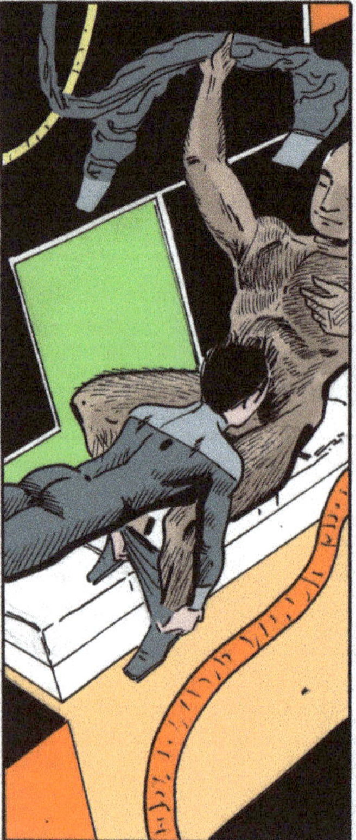
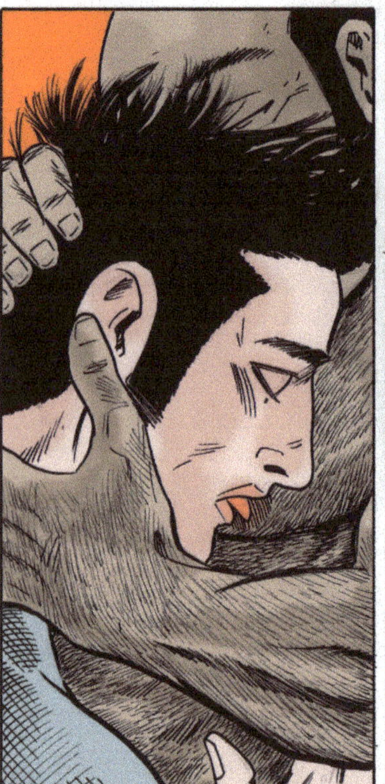

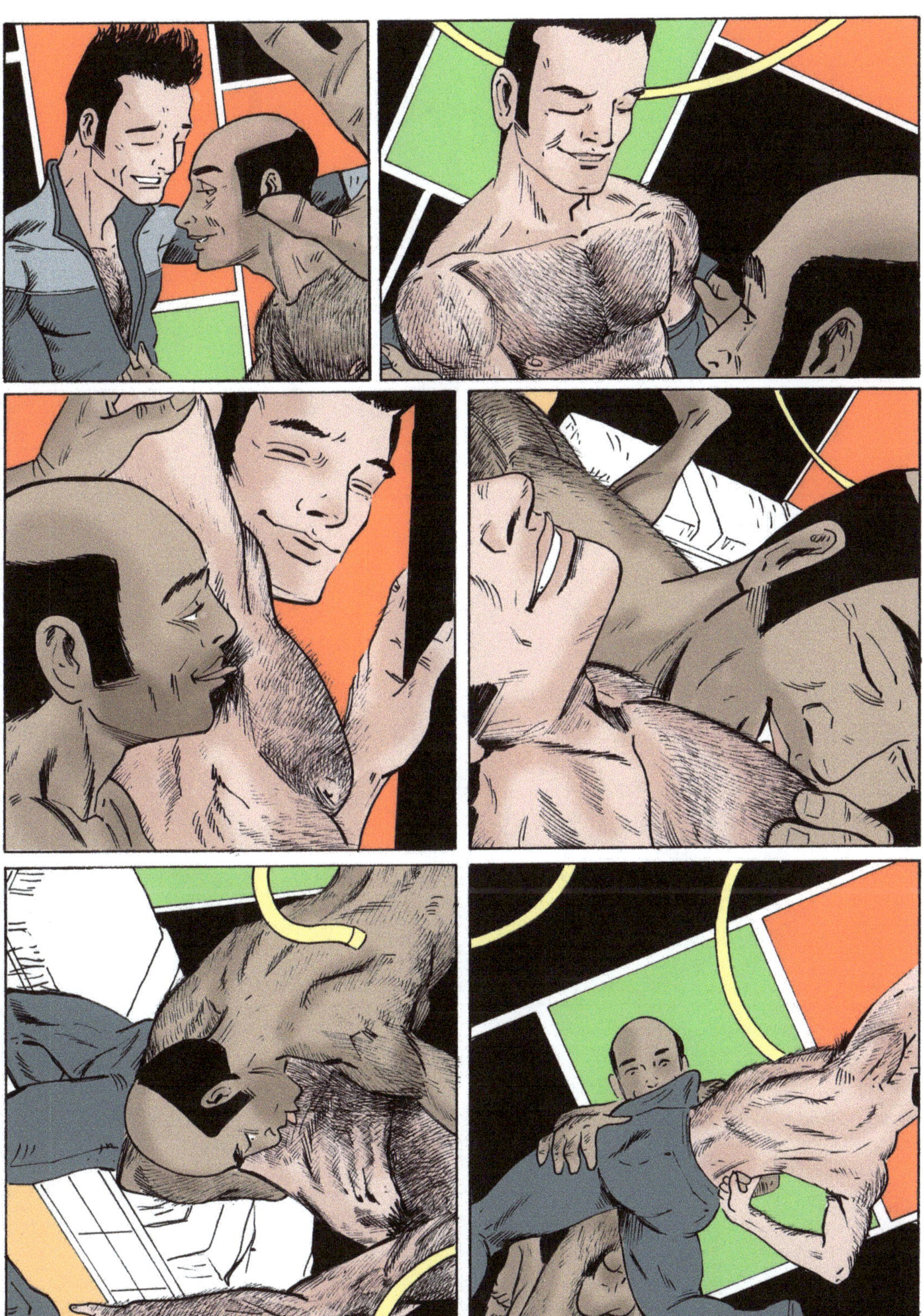

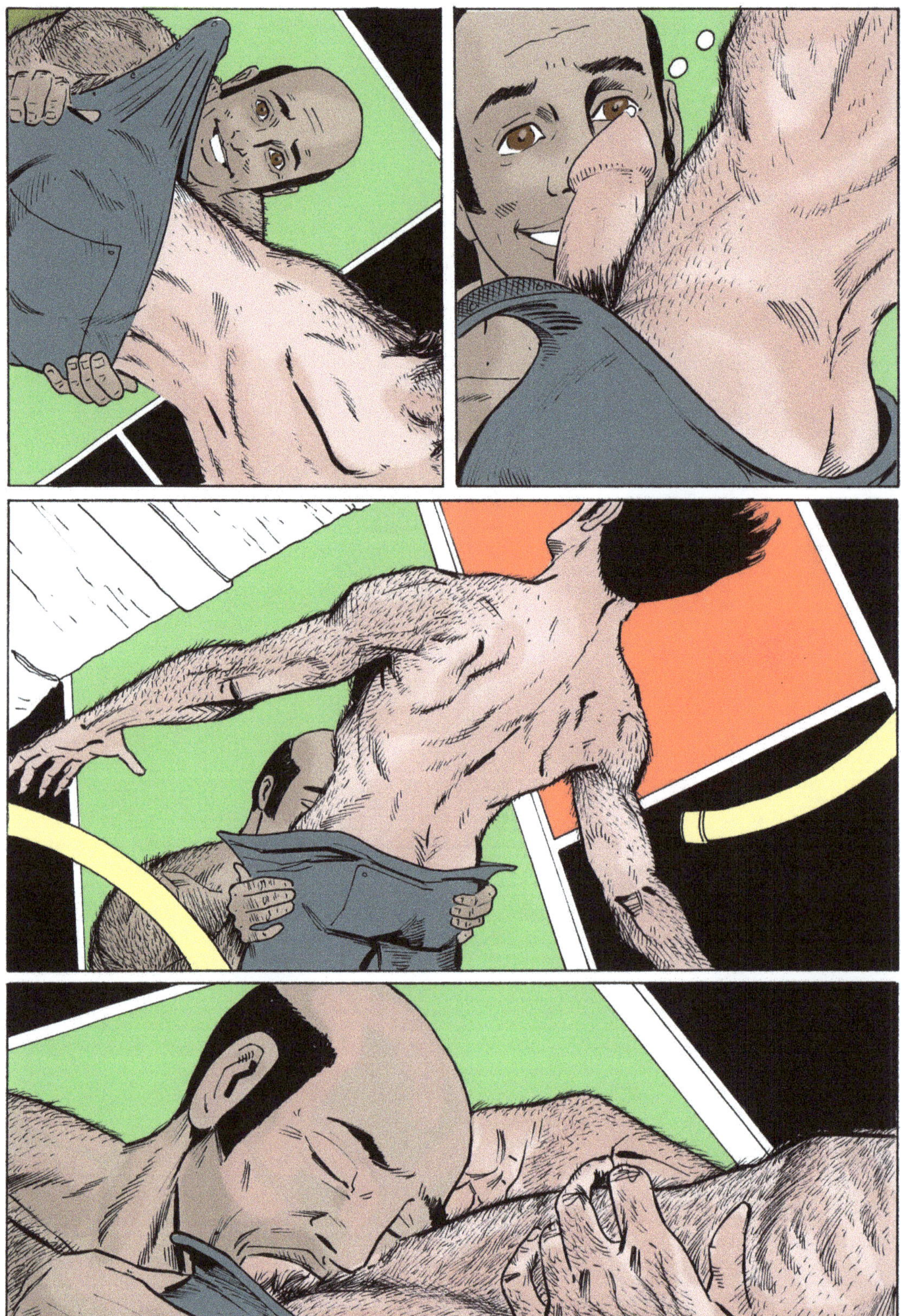

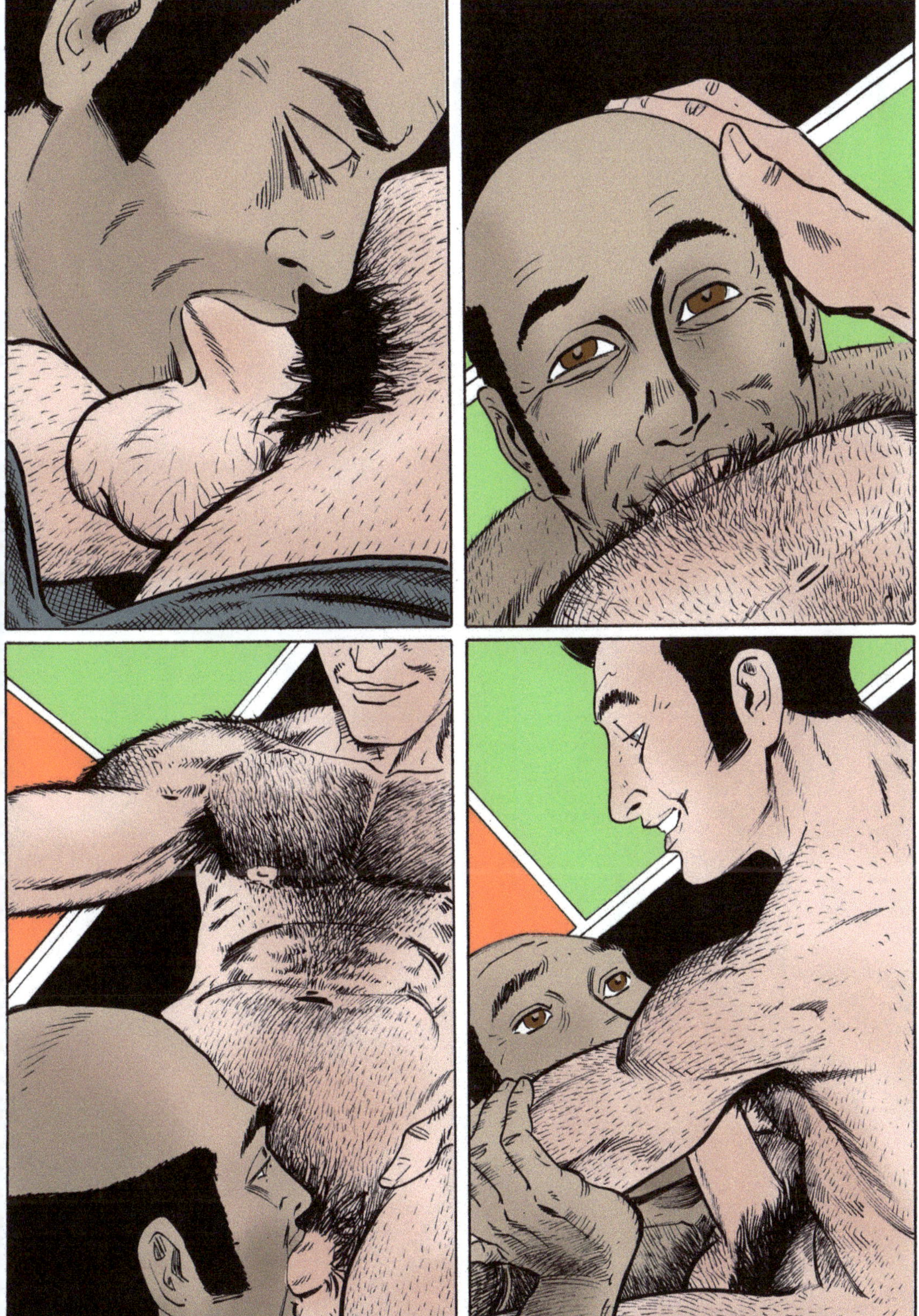

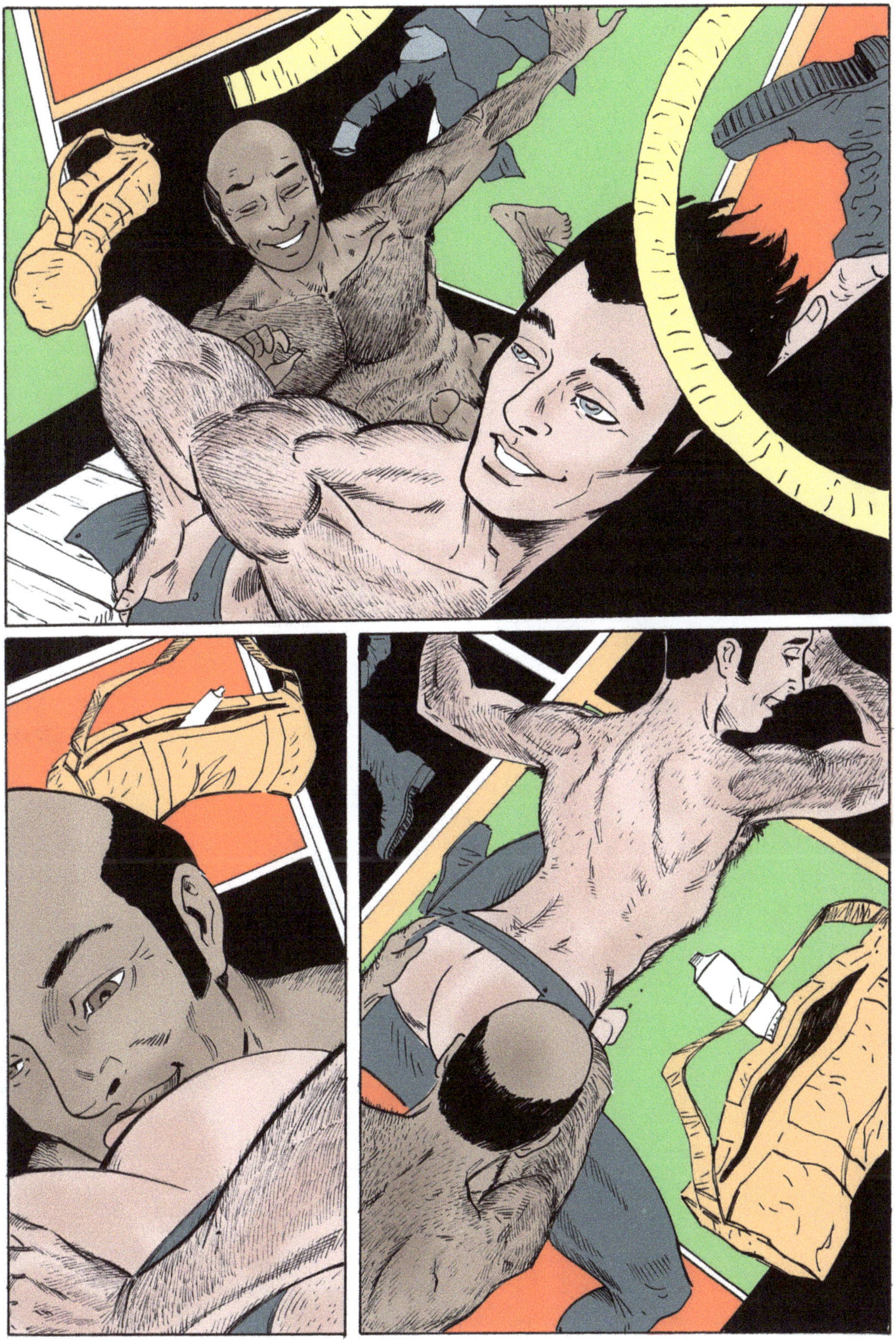

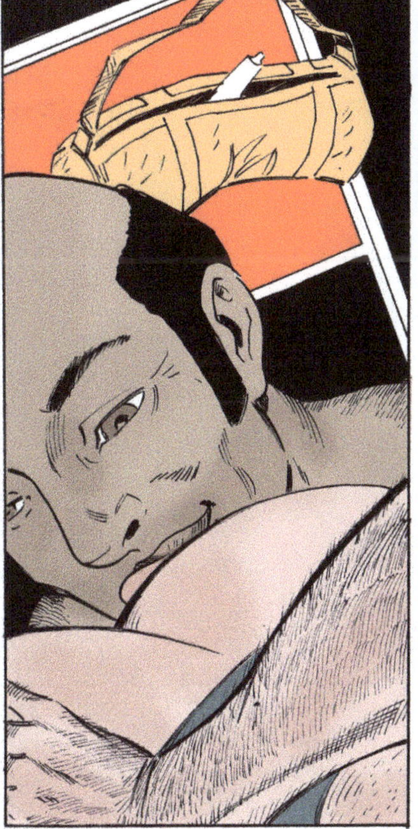

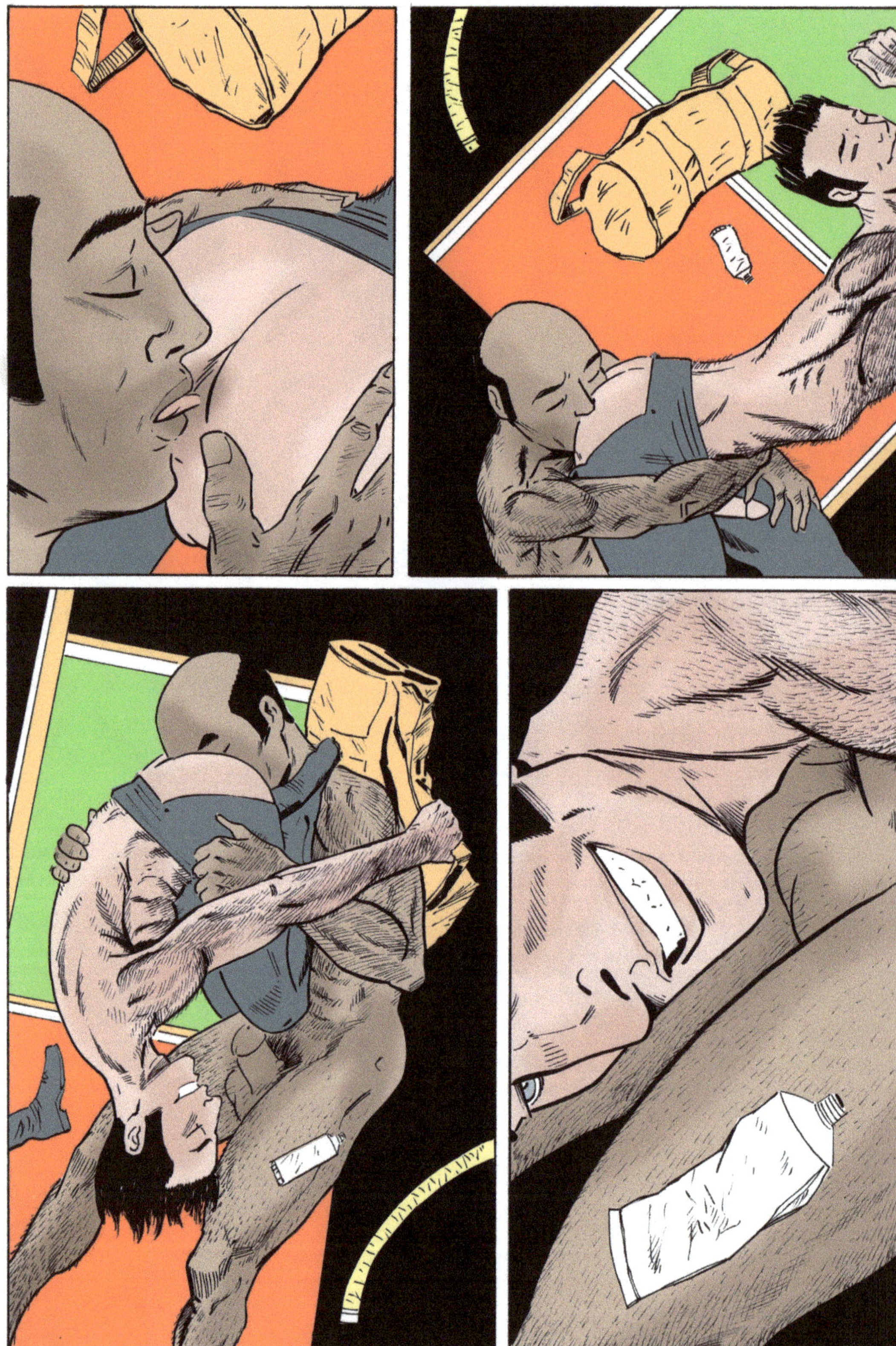

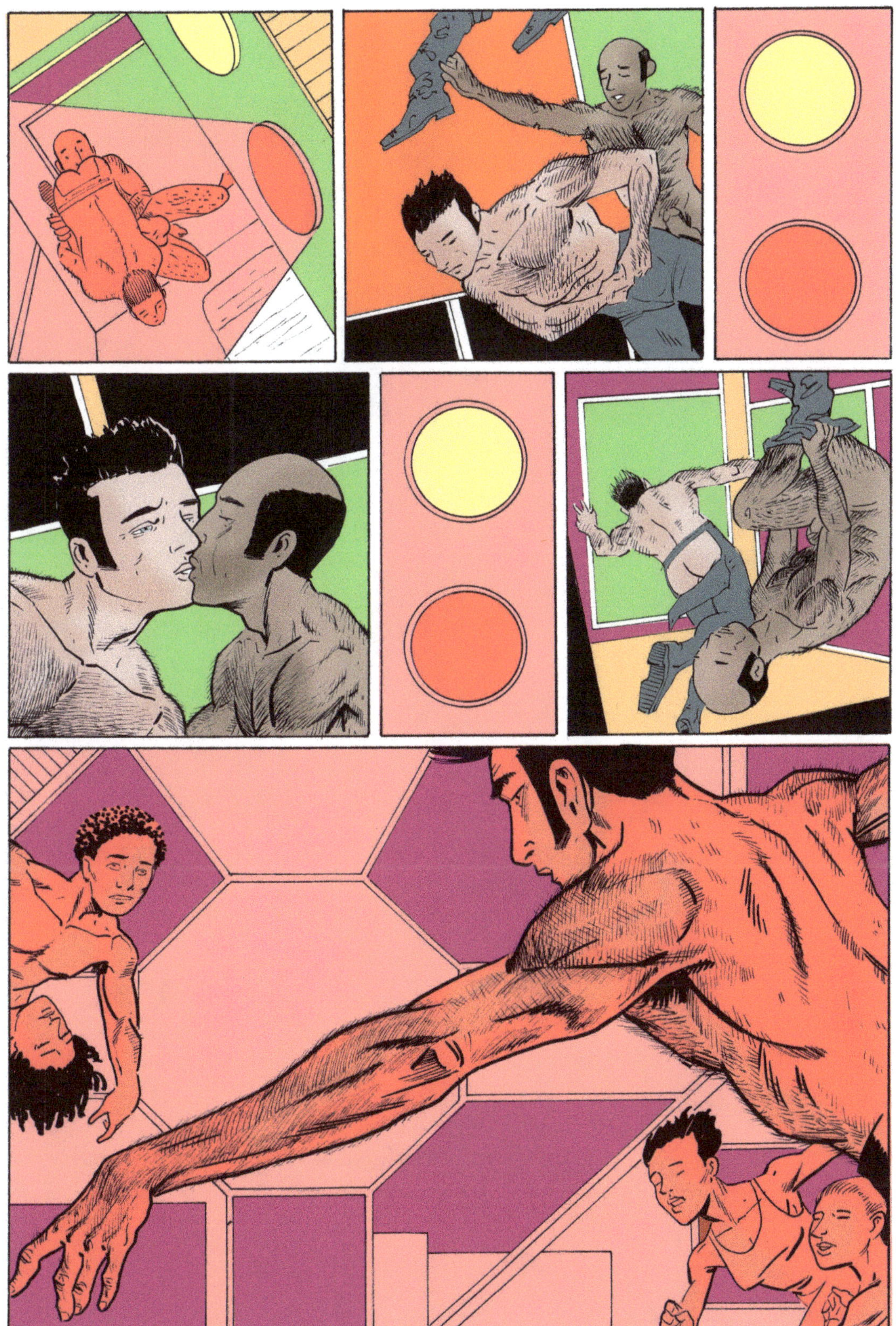

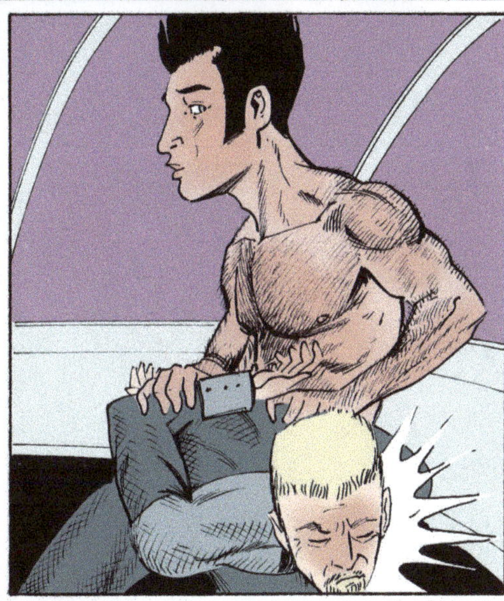

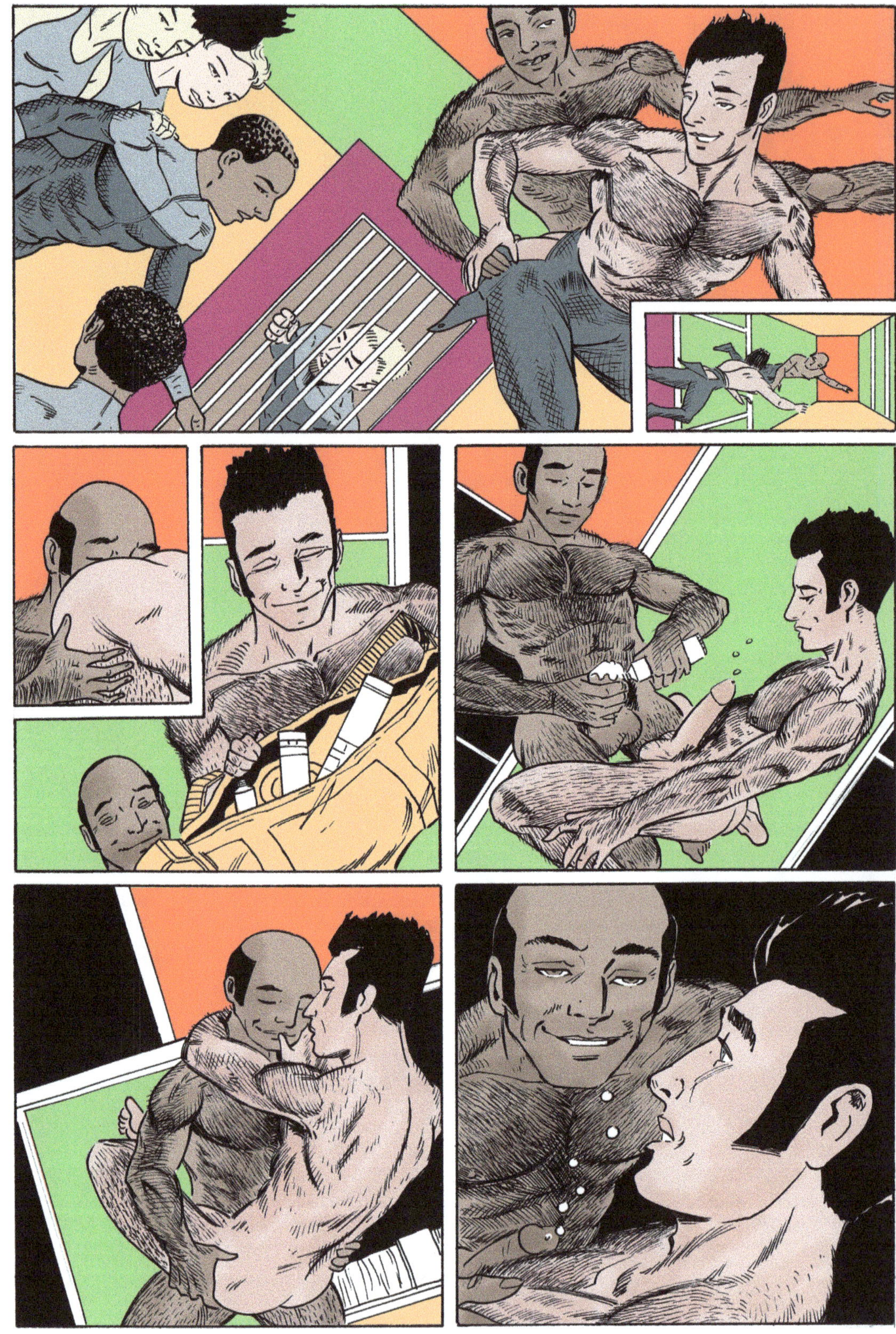

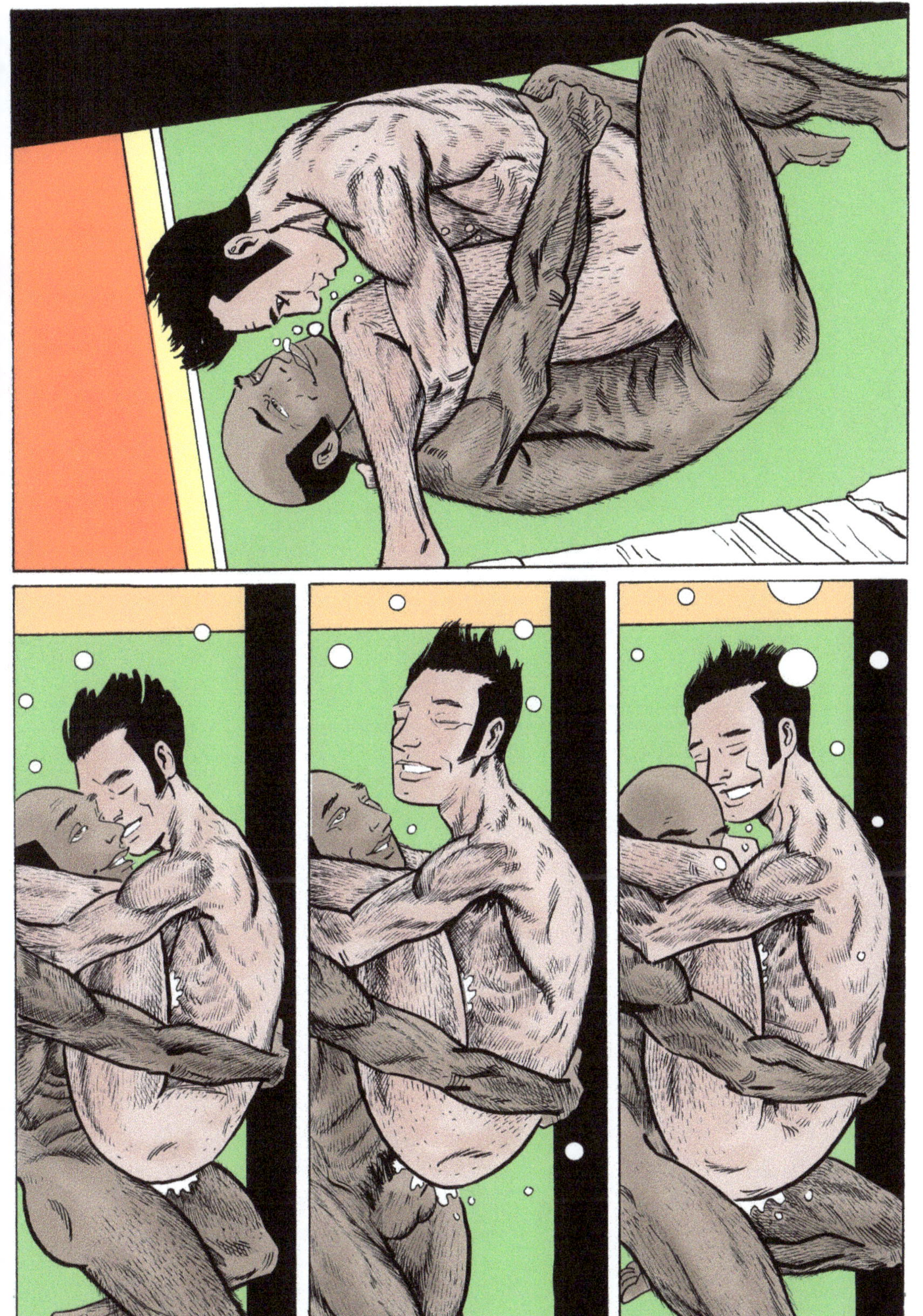

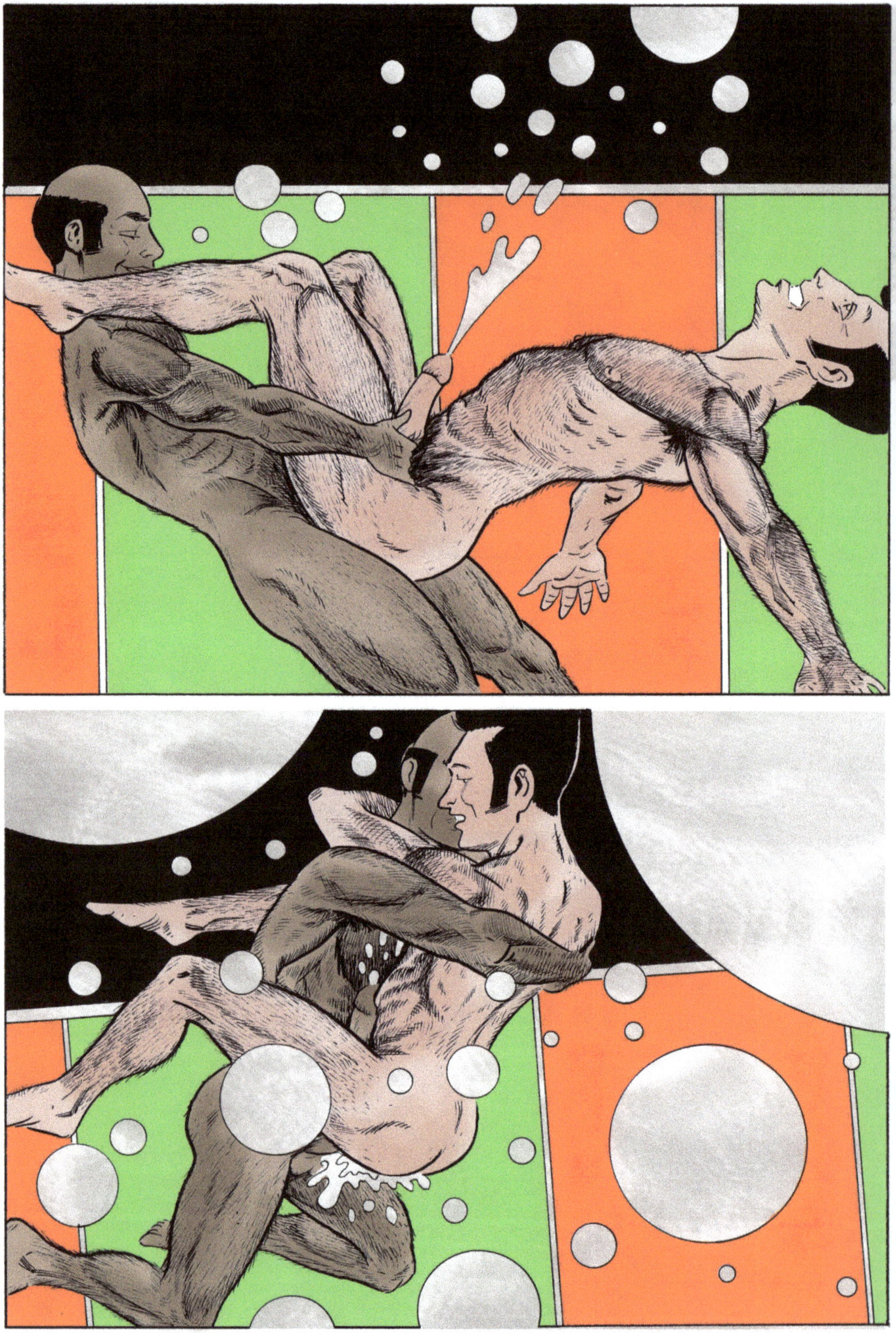

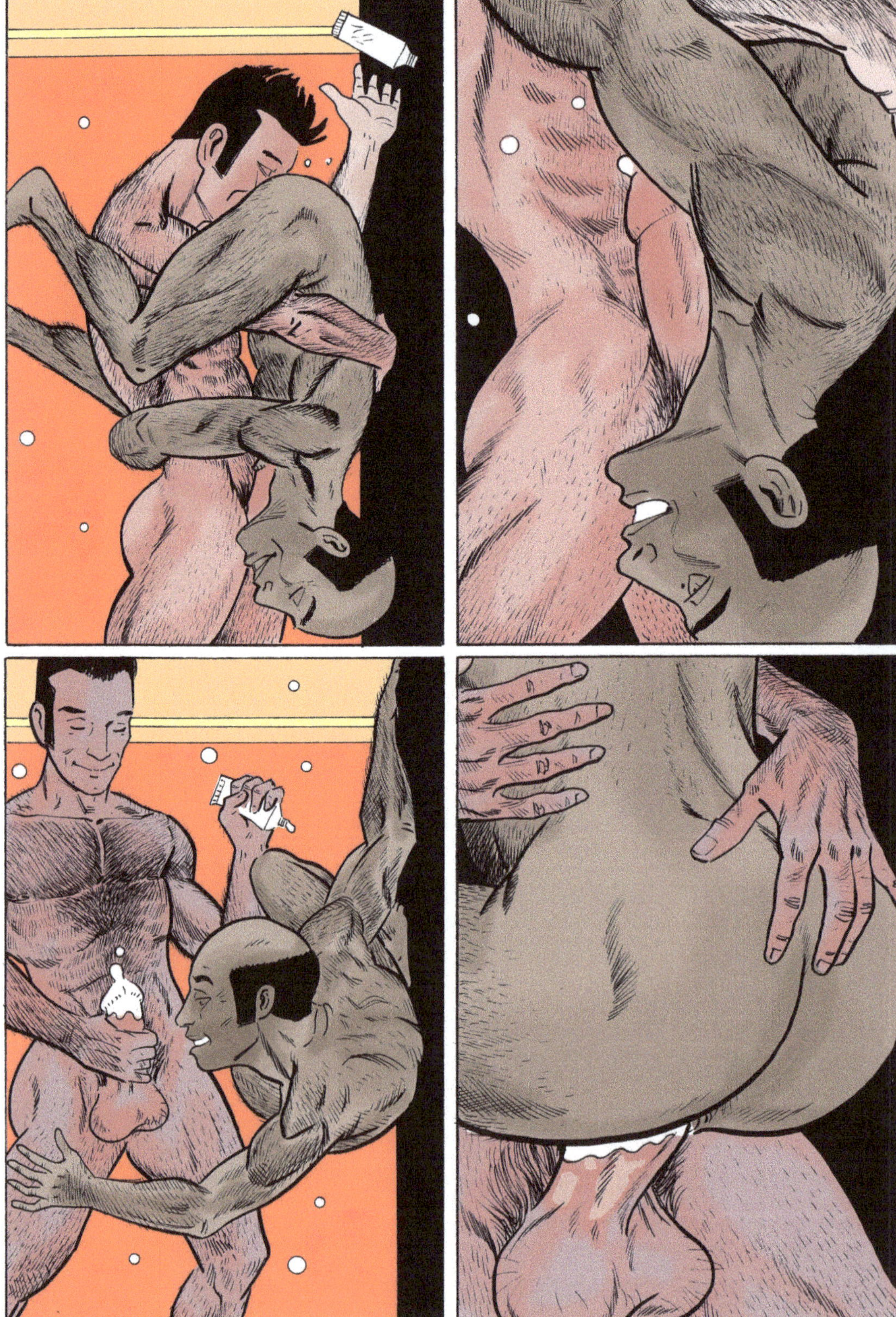

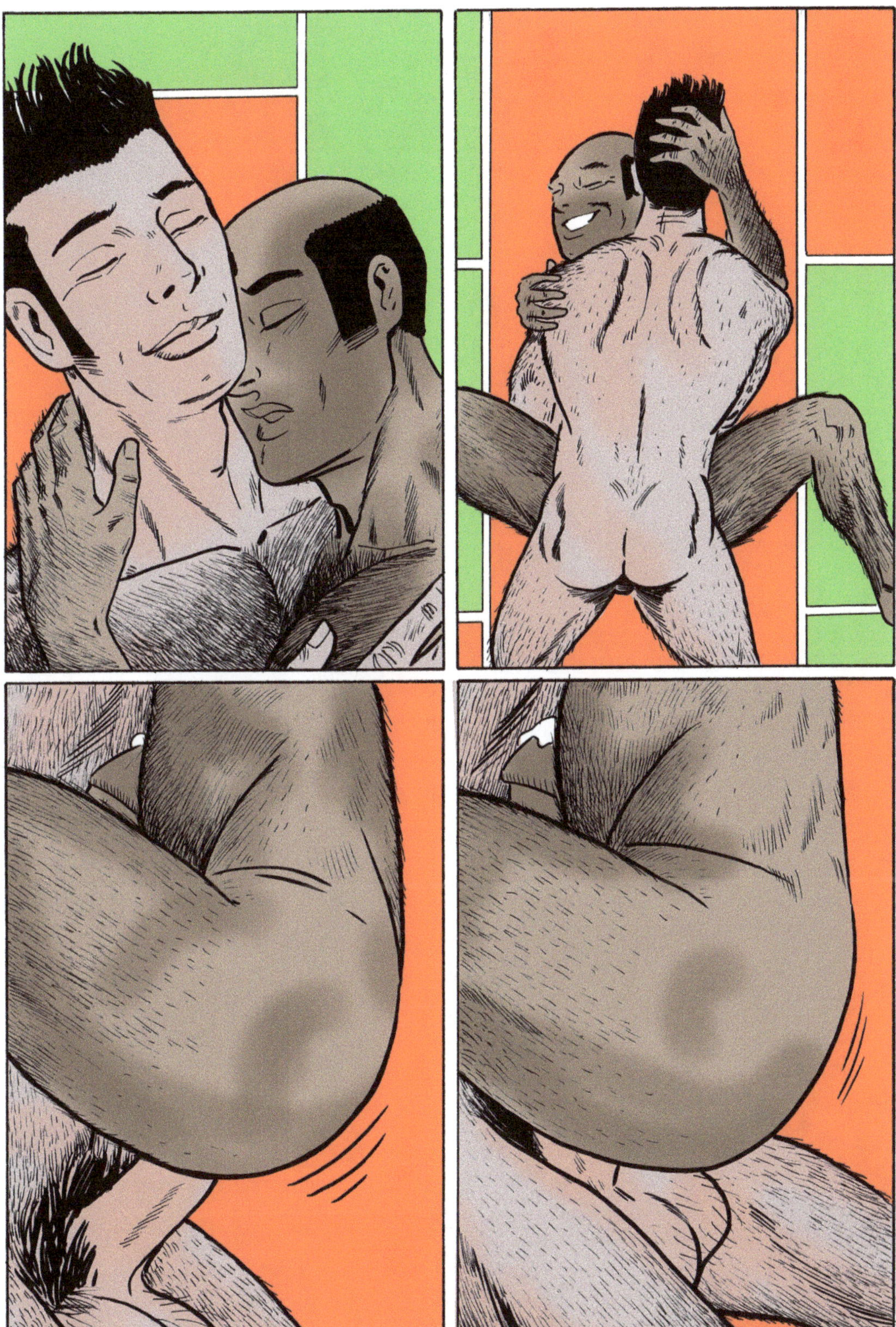

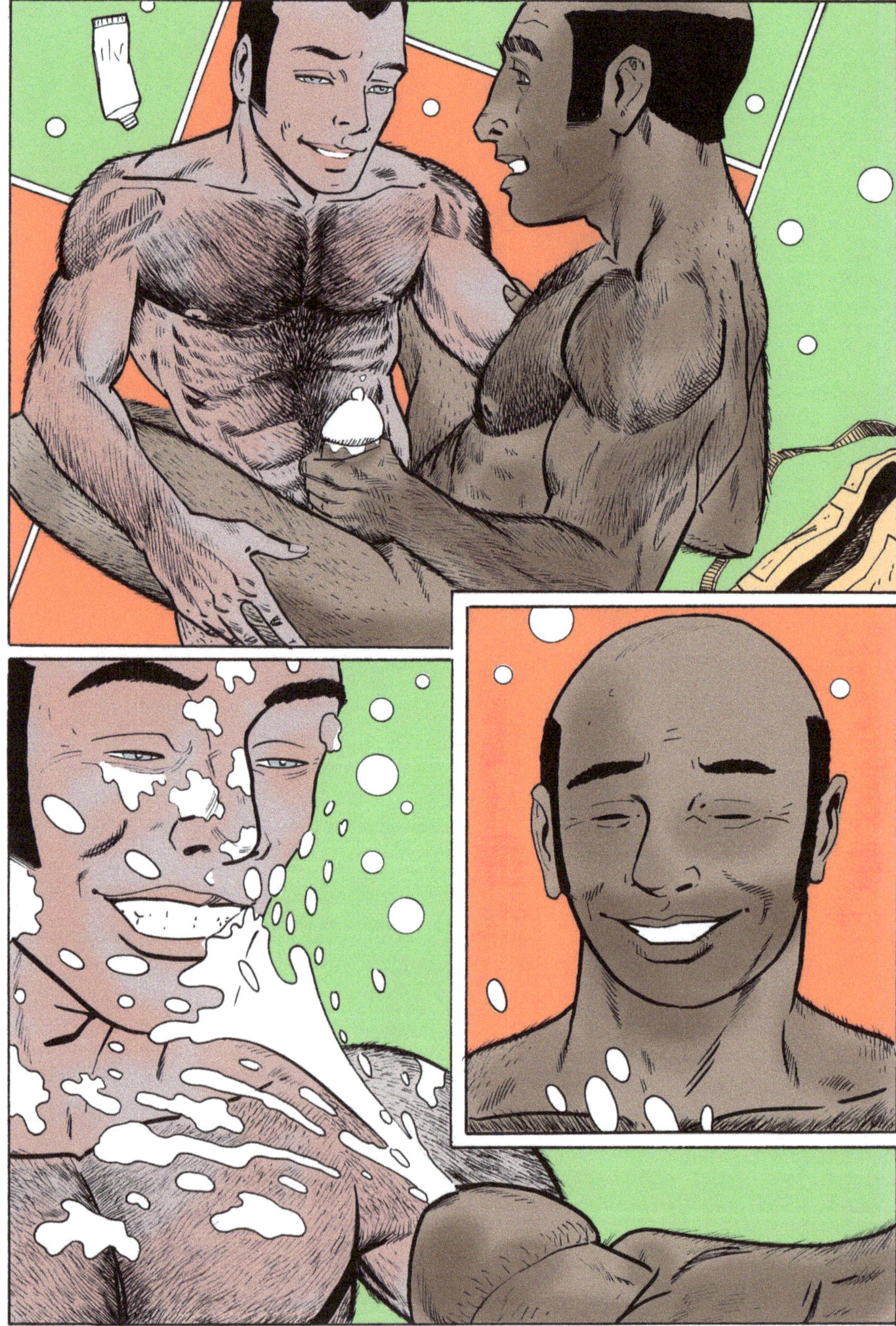

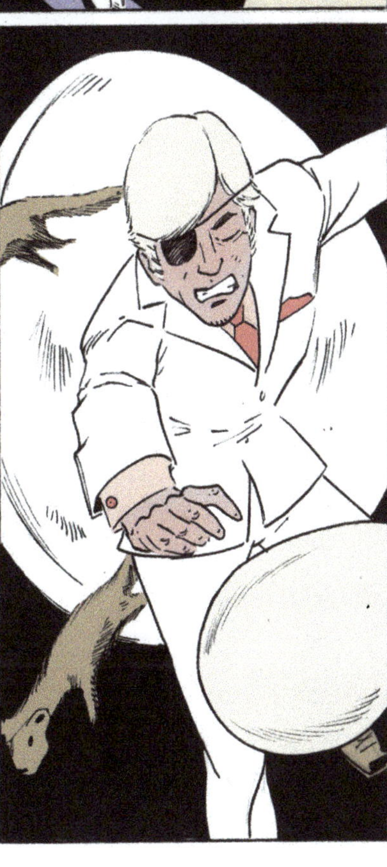

KILLER KISS

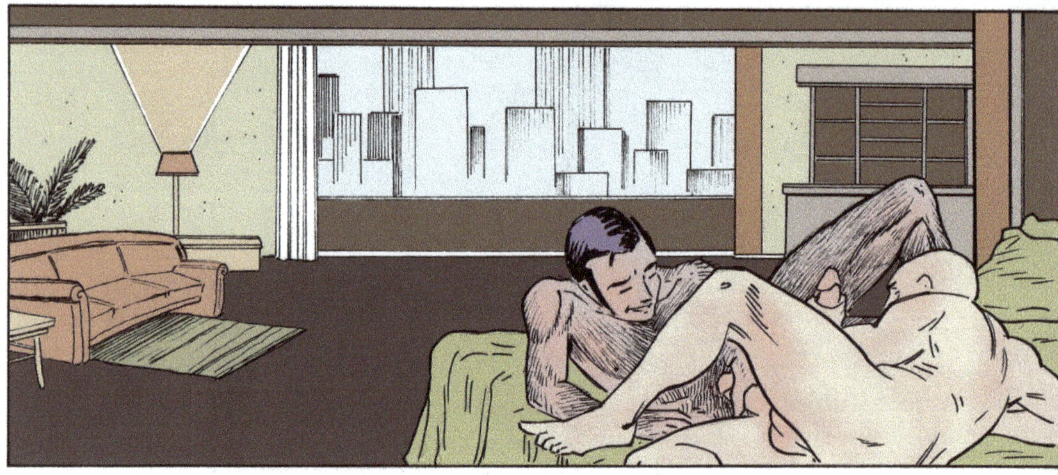
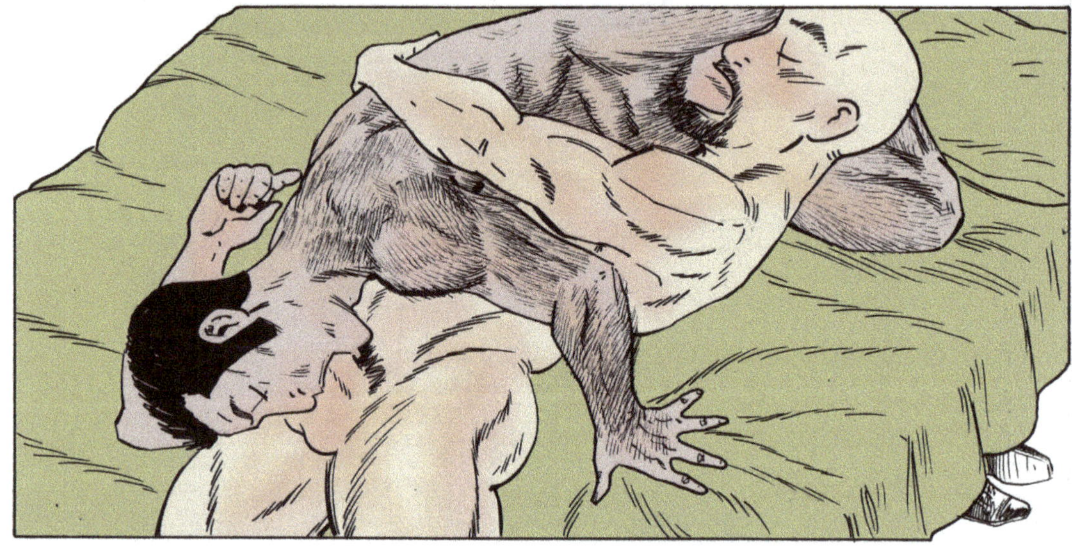

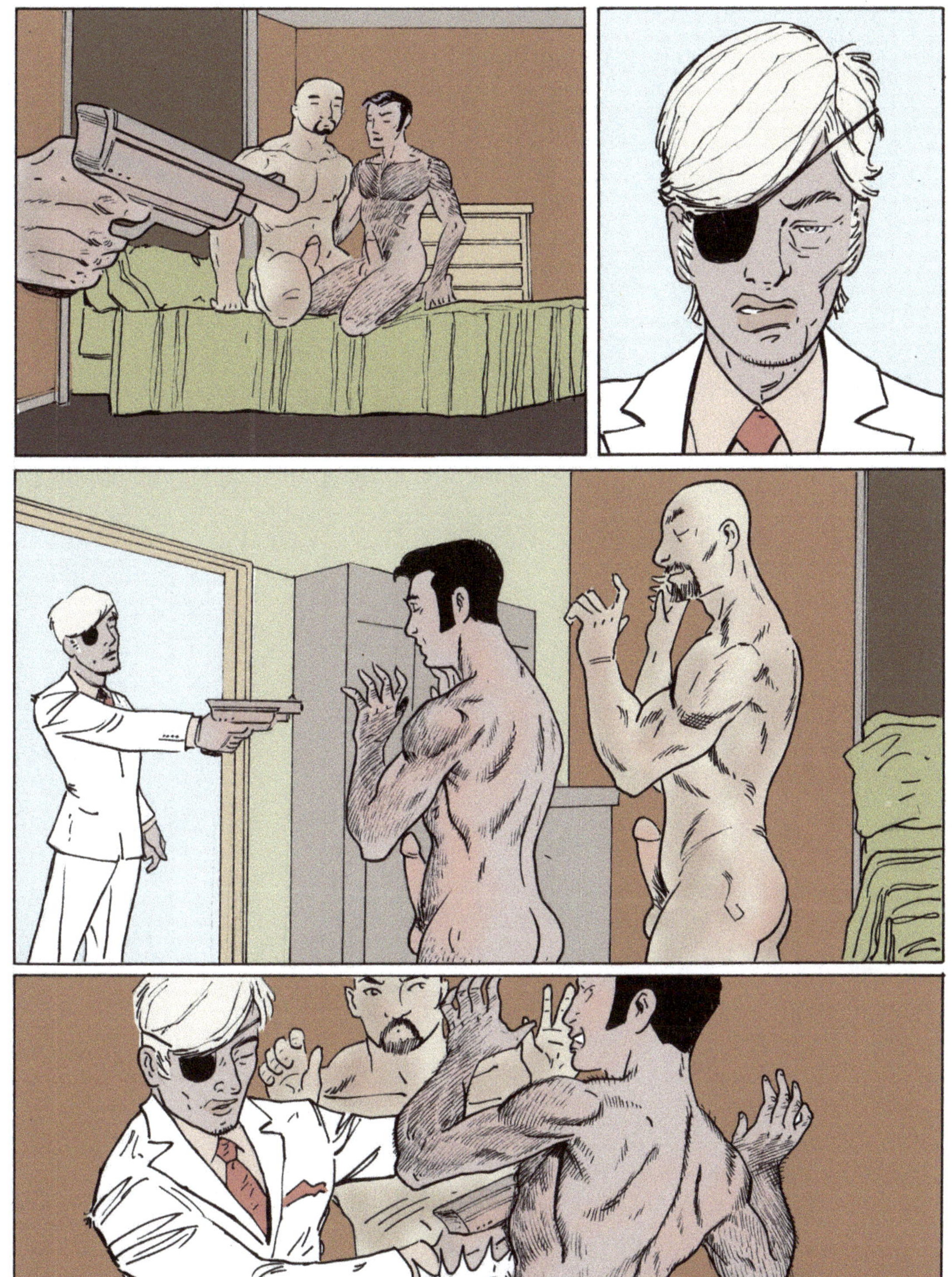

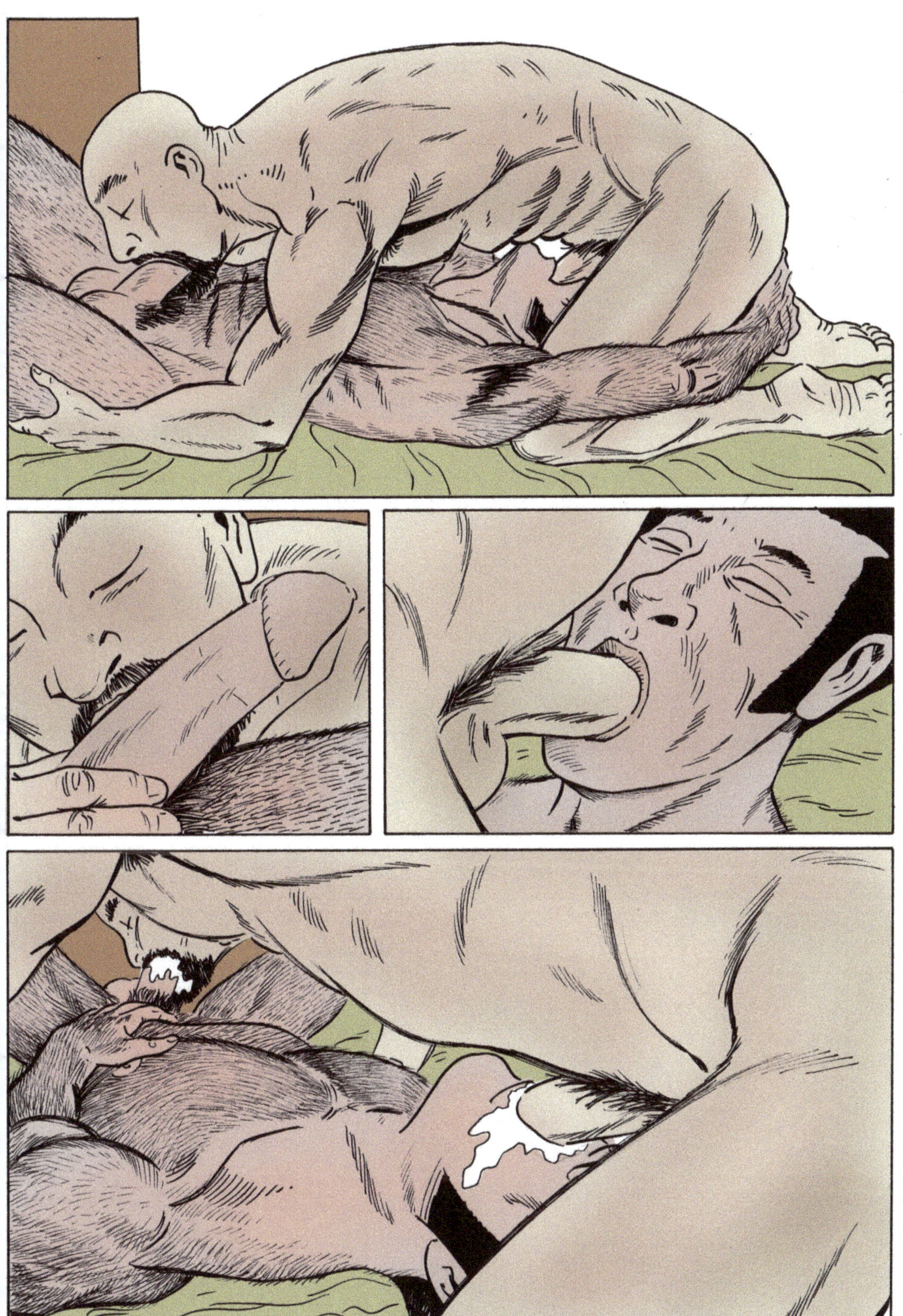

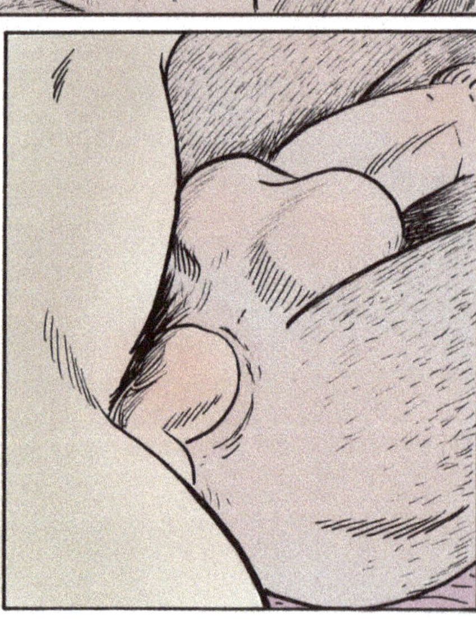

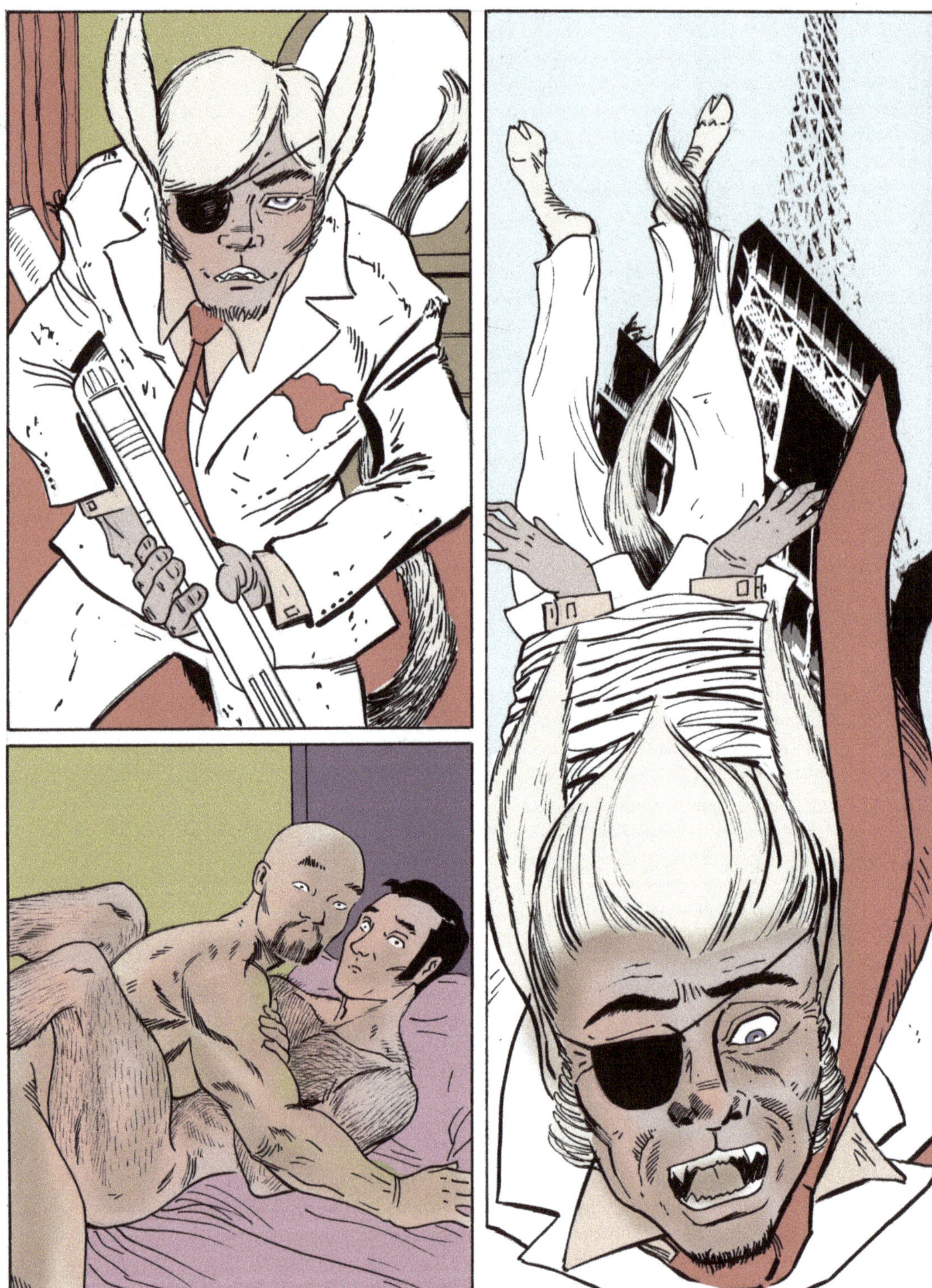

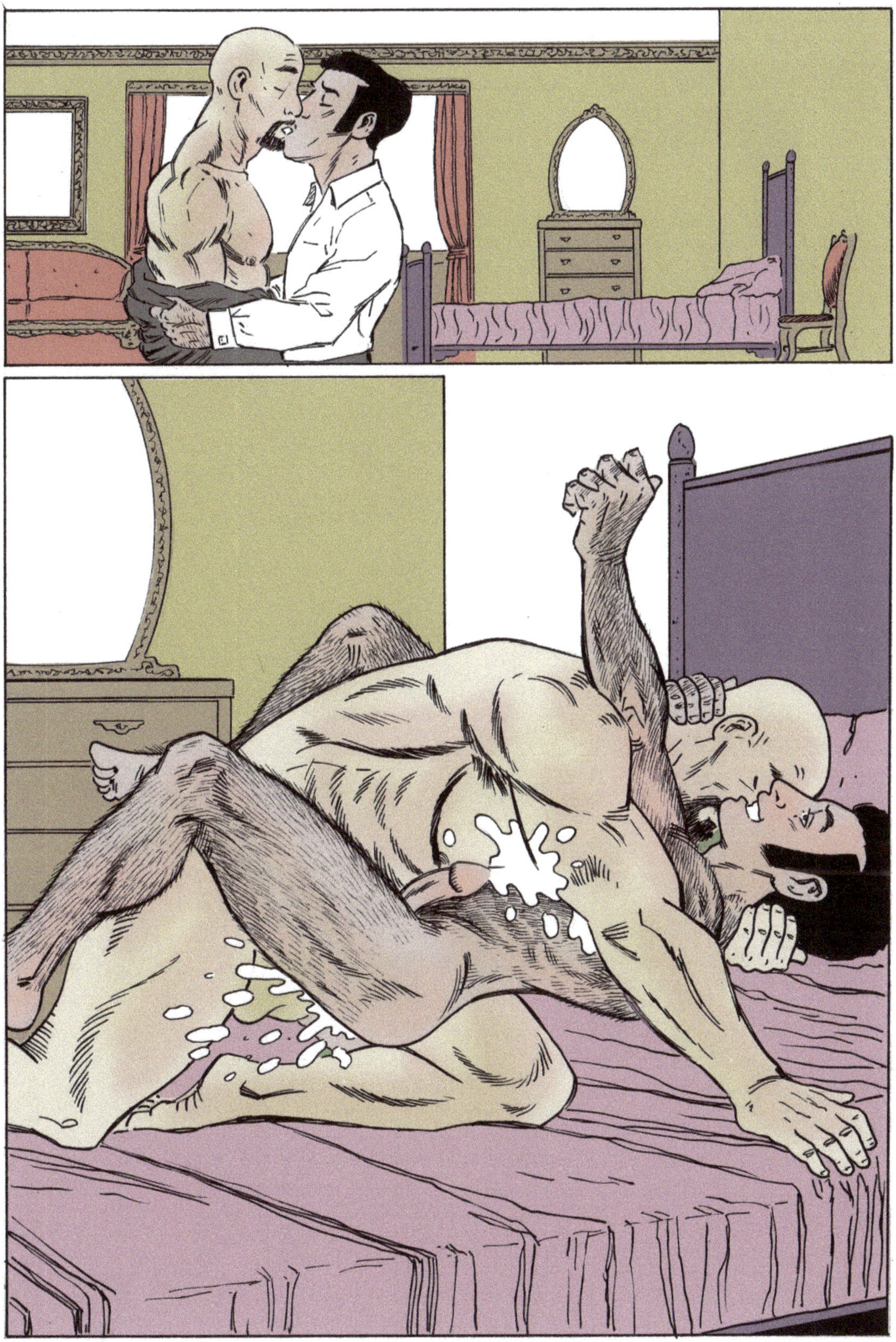

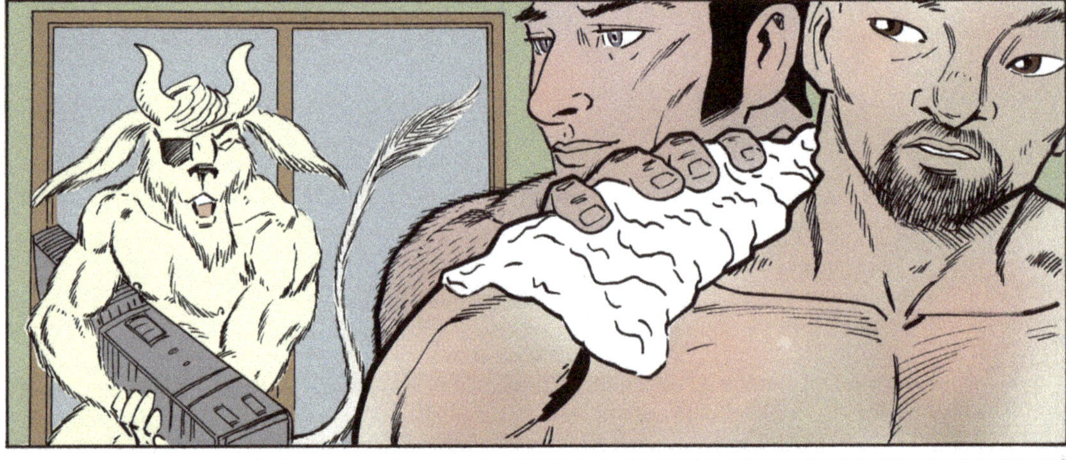

SLY

script/edits: Dale Lazarov
art/colors: mpMann

About The Authors:

<u>Dale Lazarov</u> is the writer/art director of CARNAL (drawn by theAmir), SLY (drawn by mpMann), BULLDOGS (drawn by Chas Hunter & Si Arden), PARDNERS (drawn by Bo Revel), PEACOCK PUNKS (drawn by Mauro Mariotti), FAST FRIENDS (drawn by Michael Broderick), GREEK LOVE (drawn by Adam Graphite), GOOD SPORTS (drawn by Alessio Slonimsky), NIGHTLIFE (drawn by Bastian Jonsson), MANLY (drawn by Amy Colburn), and STICKY (drawn by Steve MacIsaac) — wordless, gay character-based, sex-positive graphic novels published in hardcover by ComicMix and in digital format through Class Comics. He lives in Chicago.

<u>mpMann</u>'s comics include work on four graphic novels for Archaia Studio Press, and a wide range of mini-comics, small press comics and web comics. For a more in-depth look, a slightly outdated web site can be found at cosmorynth.com. Various and sundry interviews and reviews can be found by simply googling mpMann. Mann lives in California.